THE ...

Library of Congress Cataloging-in-Publication Data
Neumeyer, Peter F.
Donald and the— / Peter F. Neumeyer ; drawings by Edward Gorey.
p. cm.
Summary: Donald's new pet undergoes a surprising change of appearance.
ISBN 0-8109-4836-2
[1. Worms—Fiction. 2. Pets—Fiction. 3. Metamorphosis—Fiction.] I.
Gorey, Edward, 1925– ill. II. Title.

PZ7.N445Do 2004
[E]—dc22
2003013908

Illustrations copyright © 1969 Edward Gorey
Text copyright © 1969 Peter F. Neumeyer
Afterword text copyright © 2004 Peter F. Neumeyer
Published in 2004 by Harry N. Abrams, Incorporated, New York
Printed and bound in China
10 9 8 7 6 5 4 3

Harry N. Abrams, Inc. 100 Fifth Avenue, New York, NY 10011
www.abramsbooks.com

Abrams is a subsidiary of
LA MARTINIÈRE
G R O U P E

DONALD AND THE...
PETER F. NEUMEYER
& EDWARD GOREY

Harry N. Abrams, Inc., Publishers

For Helen, Zack, Chris and Dan

One day Donald and his mother,
a beautiful lady,
went to the garbage can.

At the bottom they found
what looked like a white worm.
'Oh Donald,' said his mother.

Donald looked at the white worm
and took it in his hand.
He loved animals.
'Let me keep it, Mother,' he said.

Donald's mother was as kind as she was beautiful.
She said *yes*.

She gave Donald an empty jar in which to put his worm.

Donald gave his worm greens to eat.

'Can it breathe?' asked Donald.
Donald's mother, who was also very wise,
made holes in the lid.

Donald watched his worm all that day.

'I have a new friend,'
he thought when he went to bed that night.

The next morning Donald jumped out of bed
to see his worm.
At first Donald saw nothing—only the greens,
and where the worm had been, a little brown case.

When Donald went to bed that night, he was sad.
'I will find a better worm tomorrow.'

The next day Donald had painful ribs.
His mother kept him in bed.

For a time he surveyed his room from there.

Donald constructed things.

Donald imagined things.

Then he was well.
He got up to fetch his jar.
What do you think he found inside?

The most beautiful
rainbow winged

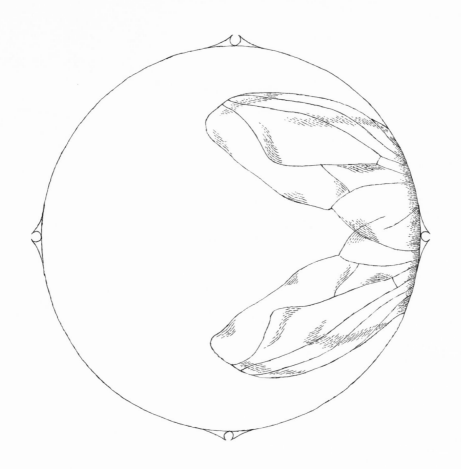

furry footed

enormous eyed

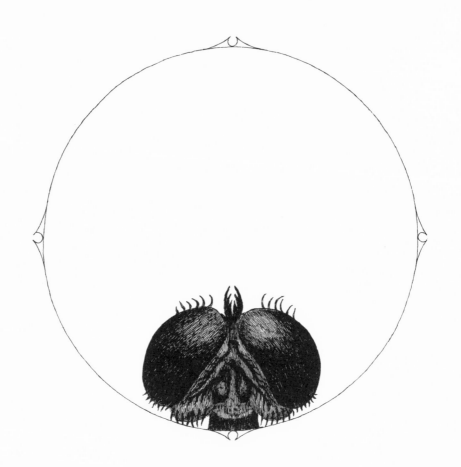

peculiar mouthed

.

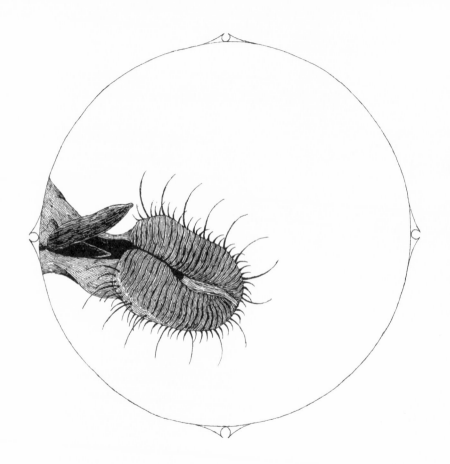

. . . housefly

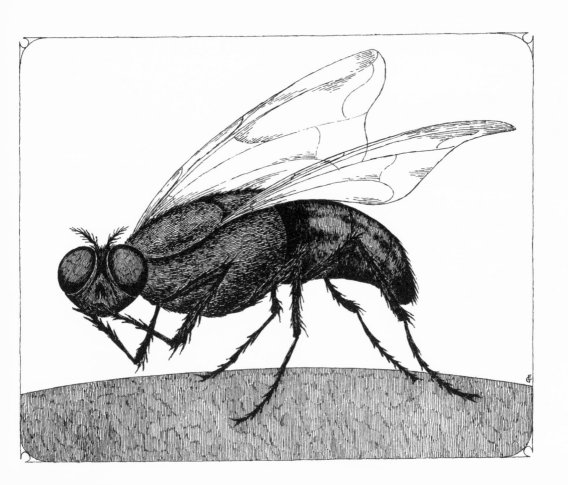

How It All Began

"You've got to meet Edward Gorey," said Harry Stanton, my editor at Addison-Wesley, Publishers. "You'll have so much to talk about," he added, employing that formula designed to make two people feel awkward when they finally do meet.

Some months earlier, in the spring of 1968, Stanton had been at my house to discuss a college textbook I was writing. I had stepped out of the room, and Harry, glancing at the top of my desk, must have seen a little watercolor book I'd painted and written that summer to comfort our seven-year-old Christopher, who had broken his leg. When I came in, Stanton said, "Forget about textbooks; let's do children's books."

At this early time, Stanton wanted to use my own amateurish illustrations, but at Addison-Wesley more prudent heads prevailed. Someone had pointed out that a fine young artist by the name of Edward Gorey had been doing intriguing book covers at Doubleday Anchor.

And so, some months later, in late summer 1968, Harry, Ted (to his friends), and I went sailing off Barnstable, Massachusetts, in Harry's boat. Ted and I sat stone silent, bow and stern, stumped for easy banter.

Blessedly, time passed. Ted and I rowed the dinghy to the dock. As Ted held the rope ("painter," Harry might've said) and stepped up on the dock, the dinghy scooted out from under, leaving Ted a-straddle, one foot on shore, one on the dinghy, which skittered away, until Ted himself fell down between. I grabbed for his arm, hooked him somehow to the dock, and took off after the dinghy that was floating out on the tide.

When I came ashore again, there was Ted, his left shoulder protruding out from his back like a bird's broken wing.

Minutes later, in the waiting room of the Hyannis hospital, we sat to wait. And we sat. And sat, until finally Ted, looking startled, turned to me and whispered, "I think it's popped back into place." As, indeed, it had.

We tried to leave. But once checked in to the Hyannis emergency room, exit is not permitted before a doctor has checked you.

Again we sat, Harry suggesting we look at the "Donald" sketches from the car trunk. We appeared an odd trio as we viewed Ted's illustrations for the first time, laughing till we hurt.

Ted, of course, was just as he has usually been described in books and interviews—a striking, tall, bearded Viking of a man, weighted with silver and beaded necklaces, fingers laden with rings—still wet and bedraggled. Incongruous in the claustrophobia-inducing waiting room, he, or we, baffled the startled citizens of Hyannis who shared our space.

Even after our rowdy perusal of the book, we weren't allowed to leave. At one point Ted went into the men's room, came out cradling a blanket, and called out, "Nurse! I've had it all by myself. Now can we leave?"

Sitting there, then, we saw for the first time Donald's mother, "as kind as she was beautiful," noted the peregrinating shoe under Donald's bed, and the umbrella-stand dragon slayer (Donald's seafaring father?) on the back cover.

As for the climactic, looming housefly, it was drawn from life. As Gorey wrote me: "[T]he fly drawing is done, and I think it looks right, despite my somewhat twitchy state, as I spent a thwarting afternoon yesterday drawing it several times and making a hash of it, . . . I add that it was a corpse before I began using it (actually I recognized him when I found him on the floor as one I had seen several days ago on a window because he only had five legs)." At the top of that letter is a little one-and-a-half-inch scrap of paper with a dot, and the designation